Nadine Titus

Karen's New Puppy

**Look for these
and other books about Karen
in the
Baby-sitters Little Sister series**

Little Sister

Karen's New Puppy

Ann M. Martin

Illustrations by Susan Tang

LITTLE APPLE
PAPERBACK

SCHOLASTIC INC.
New York Toronto London Auckland Sydney

No part of this publication may be reproduced in whole or in part, or stored in a retrieval system, or transmitted in any form or by any means, electronic, mechanical, photocopying, recording, or otherwise, without written permission of the publisher. For information regarding permission, write to Scholastic Inc., 555 Broadway, New York, NY 10012.

ISBN 0-590-26195-9

12 11 10 9 8 7 6 5 4 3 2 1   6 7 8 9/9 0 1/0

Printed in the U.S.A.   40

First Scholastic printing, April 1996

An Exciting Day

"Bye, Nancy! See you later," I called.

It was Monday afternoon, the first of April. I hopped off the school bus and raced to the little house. I had exciting news to tell Mommy.

She was waiting outside with open arms. Before I told her my news, I gave her a big hug and a kiss. I was gigundoly happy to see her. That is because it was my first day back at the little house. I had been living for a whole month at the big house.

I will tell you later why I have two

houses. First I will tell you about me.

My name is Karen Brewer. I am seven years old. I have blonde hair, blue eyes, and a bunch of freckles. I wear glasses. I have two pairs. I wear the blue pair for reading. I wear the pink pair the rest of the time.

"How was school today?" asked Mommy.

It was time for my news.

"Ms. Colman had her baby!" I said. "It's a girl and her name is Jane."

"That is terrific!" replied Mommy with a big smile.

Ms. Colman is my second-grade teacher at Stoneybrook Academy. She is the greatest. I will miss her while she is away. She is going to stay at home for a few months and take care of Jane. Then she will come back to school. Our favorite substitute teacher, Mrs. Hoffman, will take her place. (For awhile I called her Hatey Hoffman. But she turned out to be very nice.)

Mommy and I went into the house.

"Hi, Karen," called Andrew.

Andrew is my little brother. He is four going on five. He gets home from school at lunchtime.

Woof, woof! Meow! Woof, woof! Meow!

"What is going on?" I asked.

Midgie was racing around the house chasing Rocky. Midgie is Seth's dog. Rocky is Seth's cat. (Seth is my stepfather.) Midgie and Rocky usually ignore each other.

"I think Midgie has spring fever," said Mommy. "She has been a bundle of activity lately. She runs around the house, begs to play, or scratches at the door to go outside. She even got out and wandered off by herself a couple of times."

"I did not leave the door open!" said Andrew. "I was not even here."

Once Andrew left the front door open, and Midgie ran outside and almost got hit by a car.

"I know," replied Mommy. "We cannot figure out how she is escaping. The screen door was fixed. And we are always careful about closing doors."

Midgie and Rocky sped past us again. They were having an exciting race. Then Rocky slipped under the couch. Midgie sat down to wait for him to come out.

While she was waiting, I ran upstairs to say hello to my room and my things. They were just the way I had left them a month earlier.

When I finished saying hello, I ate a snack with Andrew. Then we went outside to play with our little-house friends.

They are Nancy Dawes and Bobby Gianelli, who are in my class at school (Nancy is my best friend); Bobby's sister, Alicia, who is four; Kathryn Barnes, who is six; Kathryn's brother, Willie, who is five; and the Barton kids. The Bartons are the newest kids in the neighborhood. They are Jackie, who is seven; Lynda, who is eight; Meghan, who is four; Eric, who is ten; and Mark, who is twelve. (Eric and Mark only

play with us once in awhile. They think we are babies.)

We are a big group. It takes awhile for us to make plans sometimes. One kid wanted to play tag. Another kid wanted to have a parade. Another wanted to play statues.

Then I got a gigundoly good idea. It came from a TV show I saw about houses.

"Let's build a treehouse," I said.

Guess what. Everyone liked my idea.

This was an exciting day. Ms. Colman had her baby. I was back at the little house. Midgie and Rocky were having races. And my friends and I were going to build a treehouse.

2

Three Houses

Once our treehouse was built, I would have *three* houses. Wow! First I will tell you how I got to have two houses.

I did not always have two houses. When I was really little I lived in one big house with Mommy, Daddy, and Andrew. Then Mommy and Daddy started fighting a lot. That made everybody sad. Mommy and Daddy explained to Andrew and me that they loved each of us very much. But they could not get along with each other anymore. So they got divorced.

Mommy moved with Andrew and me to a little house not too far away in Stoneybrook, Connecticut. Then she met a very nice man named Seth. Mommy and Seth got married and that is how Seth became my stepfather. So these are the people who live at the little house: Mommy, Seth, Andrew, me. These are the pets who live at the little house: Midgie; Rocky; Emily Junior, my pet rat; and Bob, Andrew's hermit crab.

Daddy stayed at the big house after the divorce. (It is the house he grew up in.) He met a very nice woman named Elizabeth. Daddy and Elizabeth got married and that is how Elizabeth became my stepmother. She was married once before and has four children. They are my stepbrothers and stepsister. They are David Michael, who is seven like me; Kristy, who is thirteen and the best stepsister ever; and Sam and Charlie, who are so old they are in high school.

I have another sister. Her name is Emily Michelle. Emily is two and a half. She was adopted from a faraway country called Vietnam. I love her a lot. (That is why I named my pet rat after her.)

There is one more important person who lives at the big house. That is Nannie. She is Elizabeth's mother. That makes her my stepgrandmother. She helps take care of everyone.

There are also pets at the big house. They are Shannon, who is David Michael's big Bernese mountain dog puppy; Boo-Boo, who is Daddy's cranky old cat; Crystal Light the Second, who is my goldfish; and Goldfishie, who is Andrew's kangaroo. (April Fool!)

Andrew and I switch houses every month — one month we live at the little house, the next month at the big house. (Emily Junior and Bob go with us.)

I have special names for my brother and me. I call us Andrew Two-Two and Karen Two-Two. (I thought up those names after my teacher read a book to our class. It was called *Jacob Two-Two Meets the Hooded Fang*.)

I call us those names because we have two of so many things. We have two mommies and two daddies, two cats and two dogs, two families and two houses.

Having two sets of things makes switching houses a lot easier. We each have two sets of toys and clothes and books—one set at each house. I have two bicycles. Andrew has two tricycles. I have two stuffed cats. Goosie lives at the little house. Moosie lives at the big house. I have two pieces of Tickly, my special blanket. I even have two best friends. You know about Nancy. She lives next door to Mommy's house. My other best friend is Hannie Papadakis. She lives across the street and one house down from Daddy's. (We call ourselves the Three Musketeers.)

So now you know why I have two houses. And soon I will have three houses. I will have more houses than anyone I know!

3

House Plans

On Tuesday afternoon I showed my friends a book I checked out of the school library about building treehouses.

"Those look pretty fancy," said Bobby.

"We need to build a simple one," said Nancy.

"Seth is an excellent carpenter," I said. "Maybe he will help us build our treehouse. Then we could make it a little bit fancy. I will ask him as soon as he comes home."

It was starting to rain. We spent the rest of the afternoon in the Bartons' basement drawing pictures of our dream houses. My treehouse had two floors and towers to make it look like a castle. It had a refrigerator in case I got hungry and a telephone in case I wanted to call a friend.

When it was time to go home, I collected everyone's pictures. I wanted to show them to Seth.

I had to wait an hour for him to come home. As soon as I heard his car pull into the driveway, I raced to the door.

Woof! Woof! Midgie was right behind me. She always runs to the door to greet Seth when he comes home.

I waved our pictures in the air for Seth to see.

"My friends and I are going to build a treehouse. Will you help us? Will you, please?" I asked.

Seth looked at the drawings and smiled.

"I would be happy to help," he said. "I had a treehouse when I was your age. It was my favorite place. We can build it in our backyard."

I ran to call Nancy. Nancy called Kathryn. Kathryn called Bobby. Bobby called Eric.

The next afternoon we all met in the yard to pick the best spot for our treehouse.

"How about that tree?" I asked. I pointed to the tree outside my bedroom window. If we built the treehouse there, I could look at it every morning when I woke up.

"It is too close to the house," said Mark. "A treehouse should be private."

"I like this one," said Willie. He pointed to our willow tree.

"Too droopy," said Kathryn.

"This tree is nice," said Nancy. She pointed to our oak tree. It was still bare from the winter. But it was a big, strong tree. Soon it would be beautiful and shady.

"That one looks perfect," I said. "All in favor, say aye!"

"Aye!" everyone shouted.

"We will need supplies," said Mark. "My parents always have some wood and nails in the basement."

"I think we have some, too," said Bobby.

"Let's all bring supplies tomorrow," I said. "I will ask Seth if he can come home early to help us start building."

Just before dinner Seth's car pulled into the driveway. I ran to the door to meet him. But something was not right. It was too quiet.

"Mommy, where is Midgie?" I called.

"I have not seen her for hours," Mommy replied.

Seth came inside and we searched the house.

"Midgie! Midgie, come!" I called.

"Here, Midgie, Midgie," called Andrew.

Midgie did not come. She was gone again. And for the very first time, she stayed out all night.

On Thursday morning, we heard scratching at the door. Midgie came trotting in looking happy as could be. We took turns hugging her.

"Thank goodness you are safe," said Seth.

"Do not leave again," I scolded her. "We

15

were very worried about you!"

Midgie sat up on her hind legs and waved her front paws at me. I bent down and pointed to my cheek.

"Midgie, kiss!" I said.

Midgie rested her paws on my shoulders and licked my cheek. She really is a very sweet dog.

4

Missing!

My friends and I worked on our treehouse every day after school and on the weekend, too. Seth helped us whenever he could. By Monday the floor of the treehouse was finished. We were ready to work on the roof. (We decided not to build any towers. Seth said it would take too long. Boo.)

While we were working, a car drove by. A big spotted dog was sitting in back. *Woof! Woof, woof!*

I covered my ears and waited for Midgie

to answer. I did not hear anything so I un-covered my ears. I still did not hear anything.

"Uh-oh," I said.

"What is wrong, Karen?" asked Seth.

"Midgie did not bark at the dog that just passed by. She *always* barks at dogs," I replied.

"You are right," said Seth. "I was too busy hammering to notice. We better go look for her."

"Midgie! Midgie!" I called.

My friends stopped what they were doing and helped my family look for Midgie. We searched the house. We searched the yard. We walked up the block and back.

"She's done it again," I said. "She's disappeared!"

"Let's stay calm," said Seth. "Last week she stayed away overnight. But she came back safely. She might do the same thing again."

Seth called the animal shelter and asked

them to be on the lookout just in case someone brought Midgie in. He did not seem
too worried.

But Midgie stayed out all night, and she
did not come trotting back in the morning the
way she had the last time. She did not come
home by Tuesday night either. On Wednesday morning she was still gone. By Wednesday afternoon, we were very worried.

Seth started making phone calls. He
called the animal shelter again. He called
some of our neighbors.

"Someone is bound to have seen her
somewhere," he said.

But no one had.

"We should make signs and post them
in the neighborhood," I said.

"Excellent idea," said Seth. "You start
making the sign. I will call the *Stoneybrook
News* and ask them to run an ad."

While Seth was calling the newspaper,
Mommy, Andrew, and I got to work. (I am
a very good sign-maker.) Here is what our
sign said:

MISSING!
HAVE YOU SEEN OUR DOG, MIDGIE?
IF SO, PLEASE CALL!

We put a picture of Midgie under the word "Missing!" We listed our phone number at the bottom. I made a beautiful border of dog biscuits and hearts.

"That should do it," I said.

We drove downtown to make copies of our sign, and we posted them around the neighborhood. Then we went home and waited for someone to call. We waited. And waited. And waited.

Finally on Friday morning the phone rang. We tripped over each other trying to answer it. Mommy reached the phone first.

"Hello?" she said. She listened for a minute. Then she started asking questions. She asked if the dog answered to the name Midgie. She asked how big the dog was. She asked if the dog had any special markings. That was when Mommy's face changed from excited to sad.

20

"No, our dog does not have a black patch over one eye. And she does not have black at the tip of her tail. But thank you for calling us," said Mommy.

The dog was not Midgie. Midgie was still missing. We just had to keep searching for her.

5

The Search

"I am going out to post more signs," said Seth. "We should put them all around Stoneybrook."

"We need a search party, too," I said. "I know where to find one."

It was Saturday morning. My family had just finished breakfast. The kids from the neighborhood would be over any minute. Andrew and I went out to the yard to wait for them. As soon as they arrived, I called for a meeting.

"Midgie is still missing," I said to my

friends. "We need detectives to find her. Who wants to help?"

"Me!!!" everyone replied.

"Great," I said.

I wished we had detective hats to wear. But there was no time to make them. Then I thought of something important.

"I will be right back!" I said.

I ran into the house and opened the refrigerator.

"Mommy, do we have bologna?" I asked.

"How can you be hungry? You just finished breakfast," replied Mommy.

"It is not for me," I replied. "I want to give bologna to my detectives. If Midgie is hiding, she will smell the bologna and come out to get some."

"That is a very good idea," replied Mommy. "We do not have any bologna. We have plenty of dog treats, though."

Dog treats were not as smelly. But they would have to do. I filled my pockets and went back outside. I handed out the dog treats and we started our search.

Nancy, Andrew, Bobby, Alicia, and I walked to the end of our driveway and turned right.

Kathryn, Willie, Jackie, and Meghan headed left.

Lynda, Eric, and Mark hopped on their bikes and circled the neighborhood block by block.

We went as far as we were allowed to go. We tried to think of all the places Midgie might be. She liked to play with the poodle who lived around the corner. And she liked a two-year-old down the street because he always dropped interesting toys or snacks in his yard. But Midge was not at either house.

We looked and looked. Then we hurried home hoping one of our friends had found her.

"I found the yo-yo I lost last week," said Meghan, spinning it up and down.

"I found a nickel and two dimes," said Bobby.

"I am sorry we did not find Midgie," said Nancy.

"Thanks for trying, everyone," I said.

I was still worried, but Seth was on the case. He was making phone calls about Midgie.

It was time for me and my friends to get back to work on the treehouse. Mommy and Seth came out every once in awhile to see how we were doing. We were doing very well.

We were using blocks of wood to make steps. We took turns lining them up and nailing them to the tree. I had just taken my turn when Mommy and Seth came running outside.

"We got a phone call from a woman who lives across town. She thinks she might have found Midgie," said Mommy.

Andrew and I said good-bye to our friends and piled into Seth's car.

In no time we were knocking on the door of a big white house. A woman came to the door with a dog in her arms. The dog was tan like Midgie. But it was half Midgie's size.

Bullfrogs. I had been so excited in the car. Now I felt worse than ever.

"Thank you for calling us," said Seth. "That is not our dog. We hope you find its owner soon."

No one called again until Tuesday evening. A family had found a dog in their yard. This one sounded like it really could be Midgie. We piled into the car again.

"Midgie, here we come!" I said.

We saw the dog racing around the yard as we pulled into the driveway. It could have been Midgie's twin. Except for its ears. This dog's ears stood straight up. Midgie's ears hang down.

We thanked the family for calling us and drove home.

"Tomorrow will be a week and a half since Midgie disappeared," said Seth. "We have to start thinking that she is probably gone for good."

6

Family Meeting

By Thursday we were all feeling very gloomy. Especially Seth. Midgie had been his dog since before he met Mommy. He had brought Midgie home when she was an eight-week-old puppy.

Mommy, Andrew, and I were sitting at the kitchen table. Seth was sitting in the den.

"Losing Midgie is extra hard on Seth," said Mommy. "It has only been a couple of months since he lost his dad."

Grandad had died in February. We loved

him so much. I think about him a lot.

I wondered what I could do to make Seth feel better. I thought about suggesting getting a puppy. But Andrew and I have asked for a puppy lots of times. I would not want Seth to think we were asking for ourselves.

I thought about making Seth a get well card. But he was not really sick. I could make him a feel better card. Then I got a very good idea. I went into the den.

"Do you want some company?" I asked.

"I would love some," said Seth.

I sat on the couch next to Seth. It was awfully quiet without Midgie around. Usually she ran around chewing a squeaky toy to let us know she wanted to play fetch. Or she rolled over at our feet and whined to let us know she wanted her belly rubbed.

For awhile, Seth and I just sat together not talking. I was happy when Andrew joined us. He sat on the other side of Seth.

"Thank you for keeping me company, kids," he said.

That night I was in bed thinking about Midgie when I heard Mommy and Seth talking downstairs. I could not hear what they were saying, but they talked for a long time. The next night after dinner, they called for a family meeting.

"It feels awfully empty without a dog in the house," said Seth. "What do you think about our getting a puppy?"

Andrew and I looked at each other. Had we heard right?

"Did you say puppy?" I asked.

"Yes, I did," replied Seth. "What do you think?"

"We always wanted a puppy," said Andrew. "But how will Midgie feel if she comes back and finds a new dog living in her house?"

"That is very thoughtful," said Mommy. "But there is a good chance that Midgie will not come back. Someone very nice may have found her and not know we are looking for her. Or it is possible that she was hurt somehow. She may even have died."

"Poor Midgie," I said. "We may get a new puppy, but I will still miss her."

"We all will," said Seth. "But even while we miss her, we can love something new."

"We were thinking it would be nice to get a puppy from the animal shelter," said Mommy. "That way we can help an animal who needs a home."

"I like that idea," I said. "I bet Midgie would like it, too."

Seth said we would go to the shelter first thing in the morning. I felt happy and sad at the same time.

7

Picking a Puppy

We were at the shelter when it opened on Saturday morning.

"Take your time choosing. When you are ready, come see me. My name is Joe," said the man at the adoption center.

We saw rows of cages. We saw big dogs, small dogs, short haired, and shaggy dogs. We saw older dogs and puppies. They were barking, yipping, and howling.

"They are all asking to come home with us. How will we pick just one?" I asked.

"We will go cage by cage," said Mommy.

"By the time we are through, we will know which one belongs with us."

We had decided to get a young puppy so we could raise it ourselves. The first one we came to was white with brown spots. He was chasing his tail. He was very funny. The next one was tiny enough to fit in my pocket. The puppy beside him was curled up in a fluffy ball, sleeping.

I knew we were supposed to look in each cage. But a puppy at the end of the row was looking right at me. Her tail was wagging. I could hear it thump, thump, thumping on the cage floor. I could not wait. I ran to meet her.

She had golden fur and big brown eyes. She poked her nose through the bars of the cage and licked my face.

"Andrew, come look!" I called.

Andrew raced to me. He reached out to pet the puppy. She licked his hand.

"I like her. Can she be our puppy?" he said.

Mommy and Seth came to see her. The

puppy ran to the back of her cage and brought us her ball. She tried to push it through the bars of the cage, but it would not fit.

"She is sweet and frisky," said Mommy.

"She looks like a golden retriever. They are wonderful dogs," said Seth. "I will ask Joe if he can take her out."

Guess who got to hold the puppy first. Me! She was cuddly and warm.

"She just came in yesterday. She'll go fast," said Joe.

"We'll take her!" I said.

"Wait just a minute," said Mommy. "This is a big decision, Karen. We have to decide together."

"All in favor, say aye!" I said.

"Aye!" Andrew and I shouted.

Mommy and Seth petted the puppy in my arms and smiled.

"Aye!" they said.

"Congratulations," said Joe. "She's a sweetheart."

We filled out adoption papers and paid

twenty-five dollars. I felt sad leaving the other dogs behind. But we were only allowed to take one puppy.

Andrew and I took turns holding our puppy on the ride home. (Seth gave us an old towel to put on our laps in case she made a puddle.)

"We need to think of a name for her," said Mommy.

"I like Wags," said Andrew. "She wags her tail a lot."

"That is a nice name," said Seth. "Let's think of a few others. Then we will decide."

"How about Goldie because she has a gold coat," I said.

"That is another good name," said Mommy.

"Joe told me the woman who brought her in called her Sadie," said Seth. "That is a pretty name, too."

"Hi, Sadie," said Andrew.

Our puppy turned her head and looked at him.

"She knows her name. I think she likes it," I said.

We took a vote and chose the name Sadie.

The moment I got home I called Nancy to tell her my exciting news.

"I am on my way!" said Nancy.

Soon Andrew and I were in the yard playing with Sadie and all our friends. Sadie knew how to fetch. And she would sit when we told her. Well, sometimes, she would.

Andrew and I were very lucky. We had the best puppy in the whole world.

8

An Awful Night

Sadie was the best puppy in the whole world. Until it was time for us to go to sleep.

"Can Sadie sleep with me?" I asked.

"No, me!" said Andrew.

"Sadie will sleep downstairs with Rocky," said Seth. "Maybe they will get used to each other that way. It would be nice for them to become friends."

So far, all Rocky had done was hiss at Sadie whenever she came near him. Sadie backed away with her tail tucked between her legs.

I gave Sadie a big hug.

"Sleep well in your new home," I said.

"See you in the morning, Sadie," said Andrew.

I was so tired I fell asleep right away. When I woke up, I felt even more tired. That is because it was the middle of the night. Something in our house was howling.

Woo-woo-woo! Woo-woo-woo!

It was Sadie. I jumped out of bed to see what was wrong. Mommy, Seth, and Andrew were just coming out of their rooms. We hurried downstairs. Seth turned on the light. As soon as Sadie saw us, she stopped howling and started wagging her tail.

Woof! Woof!

She was so excited to see us she started spinning around. When she stopped we saw the puddle she had left in the middle of our living room rug.

"No, Sadie, no!" said Mommy.

Seth picked Sadie up and put her on the newspapers we had left on the kitchen floor.

"This is where you go," he said.

"I think we need to keep Sadie in the kitchen until she learns to go on the newspaper," said Mommy.

We put Sadie in the kitchen and closed the door. As soon as we did, she started whining.

"I can stay up and play with her," I said.

"Thank you," said Seth. "But I would like you to go back to bed and get some rest. I will stay with Sadie until she quiets down."

Boo. I wanted that job. But I was very tired. I fell asleep as soon as I climbed back into bed. I did not stay asleep very long.

Crash! Bang! Woof!

I opened my eyes. It was just as dark as before. My family ran downstairs to the kitchen.

"Oh, Sadie!" said Mommy.

Sadie was running around with a dish towel in her mouth. A can of coffee must have fallen off the counter when she pulled down the towel. Her water bowl had turned over, too. There was coffee mud everywhere. It was pretty funny.

"Sadie, Sadie, silly lady!" I said.

Mommy was not laughing.

"Kids, please go upstairs. Seth and I will clean this mess up," she said.

"Good night, Sadie," I said for the third time.

"See you in the morning, Sadie," said Andrew for the third time.

"I bet we see her sooner," I told him.

It was almost light out the next time she woke us.

Woof! Woof!

The four of us marched downstairs in a sleepy line. Sadie was sitting in the middle of the kitchen. She looked happy to see us.

"Look," said Andrew. "Sadie made a puddle on the paper."

"Good dog!" said Mommy.

"The first night can be difficult for a puppy in a new home. But Sadie will learn fast," said Seth.

"Who is ready for breakfast?" asked Mommy.

We all were. We had given up on sleeping. But we had not given up on Sadie. She had given us an *awful* night. But she was still the best puppy in the whole world.

9

What a Mess!

"Rise and shine, Karen," said Mommy.

It was late Sunday morning. I was rising. But I was not shining. I had gone back to sleep after breakfast. But I was tired from waking up so much during the night.

I ate another breakfast of Krispy Krunchy cereal. (That is my favorite kind.) Then I went outside to see if any of my friends wanted to work on the treehouse.

Andrew and the other little kids had been invited to a birthday party, so just the big kids came to help. That was probably a good thing. I was starting to worry about the little kids getting hurt around the tree-house before it was finished.

"We need to put sides on our treehouse," said Lynda. "Do you think Seth can help us today?"

"I do not think so," I replied. "He is kind of tired."

Seth had been up more than any of us with Sadie. And he was going to be spending a lot of time training her.

"We can put up the walls ourselves," said Mark. "We just have to put these pieces of wood over here. And those pieces there. The nails can go somewhere in here. It will be easy."

Mark was pointing all over the place. I do not think he knew what he was talking about.

"Let's do it," said Bobby.

We carried a big board up the steps to the platform. It was too short for one side and too long for the other.

We climbed back down and found another board. It was a good thing our tree-house was not far off the ground. The second board did not fit either. We climbed up and down three more times. We could not figure out which boards went where.

"Instead of putting up sides, we can make railings. Railings are good, too," said Nancy.

Seth had made a neat pile of wood we could use if we wanted railings. Each piece was just the same size.

"We can start at this end and work our way around the platform," I said.

We took turns holding and hammering. The first railing was a little lopsided. But I did not think it would matter when the rest of the railing was in place.

"Next piece!" said Mark.

We started an assembly line. Two kids carried the wood up to the platform. Two kids held the wood in place. Four kids took turns hammering.

Get the wood. Hold the wood. Hammer, hammer, hammer. Get the wood. Hold the

46

wood. Hammer, hammer, hammer. We were working fast and well.

Finally all the railings were up on one side. We stepped back to admire our work.

Uh-oh. Some pieces were high. Some were low.

"How did that happen?" I asked. "They were all the same size when we started."

"Um, I think I hear my mom calling," said Mark.

"I just remembered homework I forgot to do," said Jackie.

"My cousins are coming over later. I have to clean my room," said Kathryn.

Everyone was gone in a flash. It was just me and the treehouse.

Boo and bullfrogs. The treehouse was a mess!

10

Big Trouble

"Mommy, where are my sneakers?" I asked.

It was Monday morning. I was trying to get ready for school.

"There is a pile of shoes in the kitchen. Sadie has been stealing them and chewing them up," replied Mommy.

I went downstairs in my stocking feet to find my sneakers. They looked a lot different from the last time I had seen them. The right one had a hole at the toe. Half the left shoelace was missing.

"Bad dog, Sadie!" I said.

Sadie tucked her tail between her legs and slunk out of the room.

"She is not really a bad dog," said Seth. "She is just being a puppy."

"She is being a puppy on the living room rug again!" called Andrew.

"Sadie, no!" scolded Mommy. "Seth, please take her outside."

Seth ran for Sadie's leash. Just then Sadie came trotting back into the kitchen.

Me-ow! Hiss! Rocky had been sitting under the kitchen table. He did not like it when Sadie came near him. Sadie had tried to play with him a few times. He was in no mood for playing with a silly puppy.

Rocky jumped up on the table to get away from Sadie. Sadie must have thought he was playing a game. She put her paws up on the table. Rocky swatted her nose with his paw. He scratched Sadie with his claws.

Sadie started howling. *Woo-woo-woo!*

Rocky answered her. *Me-ow! Hiss!*

Sadie howled. *Woo-woo!*

Rocky answered. *Hiss!*

"We are going to have to keep them apart," said Mommy.

"Come on, Sadie," said Seth. He put on her leash and took her outside.

Rocky jumped down from the table. On the way he knocked over Andrew's cup. Milk was dripping everywhere. Rocky lapped it up as it fell to the floor.

Things were not going the way we thought they would. Sadie was getting livelier by the minute. And she and Rocky were not getting along.

I was happy when the school bus arrived. Being in school would be peaceful compared to staying home with Rocky and Sadie.

My friends and I were looking forward to working on our treehouse after school. But it was raining. So Andrew and I stayed inside. We spent almost every minute trying to keep Rocky and Sadie apart. We opened doors and closed doors. We picked up food dishes and put them down. We took Sadie outside and brought her back in.

Finally I went to my room and closed the door. I plopped down on my bed with Goosie.

"Sadie is a nice puppy, Goosie," I said. "But she is turning out to be big trouble."

Just then a little black nose poked through my door. (I must not have closed it tightly.) Sadie came bounding into the room. She ran straight to Emily Junior's cage. She put her paws up on the table and started barking. Emily Junior ran into a corner. She looked terrified.

"No, Sadie, no!" I shouted. I scooted her out of my room and closed the door. I closed it tightly this time so she could not sneak back in. Then I picked up Emily Junior and stroked her until she calmed down.

"I am sorry you got scared," I said.

I decided that bringing Sadie home to live with us might not have been such a good idea.

11

A New Home for Sadie

Things were not much better by Wednesday.

It is true that Sadie was a fast learner. Seth had taught her to sit. She would even come when we called her — sometimes.

But she was still a puppy. That meant she chewed our things, bothered Rocky, woke us up at night, and made puddles all over the house.

We had a family meeting at breakfast. Sadie was lying at Seth's feet while we talked. She was on her leash so she would not get into trouble.

"Sadie is a wonderful puppy," said Seth. "But Mommy and I have been thinking that she might not be the right pet for our family. We were wondering how you kids felt."

"I do not know how Andrew feels," I replied. "But Goosie and I were thinking the very same thing."

"Sadie makes me sleepy," said Andrew. "And she makes Rocky grouchy."

"We think she would do better in a big family," said Mommy. "A big family could give her the attention she needs. They could walk her and play with her more. If she were outdoors and entertained she would not have the time or energy to get into trouble."

"She is a real handful for a family with another animal. A family with no other pets would be best," added Seth.

"We think it is time to find a new home for Sadie," said Mommy.

Sadie looked up at us with her big brown eyes. I would be sorry to see her go. But if she could be happier with another family it would be the best thing.

Beep, beep. Andrew's car pool had arrived to take him to preschool. My bus would be arriving any minute.

"We will talk more about our plans for Sadie at dinnertime," said Seth.

After school my friends and I worked on our treehouse. Sadie was her happy, energetic self. She did not know yet that she would be moving to a new home. She was having fun stealing our wood, tugging our pant legs, and grabbing our shoelaces.

"Sadie is such a funny dog," said Jackie. "I just love her."

Hmm.

Jackie threw Sadie's ball to her. Sadie brought it right back.

"Good girl!" said Jackie.

Jackie threw the ball over Sadie's head to Mark. Sadie ran to Mark to get the ball. Mark threw the ball to Eric. Sadie ran to

Eric. Eric threw the ball to Lynda. Lynda threw the ball to Meghan. Meghan gave Sadie a turn to catch the ball. The Barton kids made a circle. Sadie ran round and round inside it.

"I wish we could have a puppy like her," said Lynda.

"You can!" I said. "You can even have Sadie!"

I told them how we thought Sadie would be happier living with a big family.

"This is great," said Mark. "But we are going to have to ask our parents."

"They did promise we could have our own pet someday," said Jackie. "Maybe they will let us have Sadie."

That night, Mr. and Mrs. Barton talked to Mommy and Seth a few times on the phone. Finally they came to our house to meet Sadie. She jumped up and licked each of them hello.

"I grew up with a golden retriever," said Mr. Barton. "I think she will make a great pet for our family."

Mrs. Barton agreed. The next thing I knew, we were packing up Sadie's things and handing over her leash. We hugged her good-bye. Then she went off with the Bartons with her tail wagging.

The minute she was gone, I breathed a sigh of relief. I was going to miss Sadie. But I was not worried about her. I could see she was going to be very happy in her new home.

12

Treehouse War

On Thursday afternoon all the kids showed up to work on the treehouse.

"Can Seth help us this afternoon?" asked Eric.

"He will not be home from work until late. He has to make up the time he lost training Sadie," I replied.

"Too bad," said Bobby. "We need a roof on the treehouse. But the roof will be even harder to make than the railings. And we did not do so well with those."

"I like our railings," said Andrew. "They are not like anyone else's."

This was true.

"I do not think we should work on the roof today. Not with the little kids around. They could get hurt," I said.

Everyone looked at me. I guess I sounded bossy. Well, someone had to be in charge. And it was my yard.

"We may be littler than you," said Meghan. "But we are not babies."

"Oh, all right. Just be really careful," I replied.

Meghan stuck her tongue out at me. I did not stick my tongue out at her. That is because she is four and a half and I am seven.

"Maybe we could paint the treehouse today," said Kathryn. "We have lots of paint. And we want it to look beautiful."

This was a good idea.

"All in favor say aye!" I said. (Even though it was Kathryn's idea and not mine.)

"Aye!" everyone replied.

We decided to paint each wall a different color on the outside. Inside we would paint pictures. (My friends and I are very good artists. We once painted a prize-winning panel on a big fence.)

By dinnertime on Thursday we had finished the outside walls. One was red. One was green. One was yellow.

On Friday we worked on the pictures inside.

"I need red paint," said Alicia.

"There is no more up here," said Bobby. "You will have to go down and get it."

Alicia climbed down the treehouse steps. The red paint was at the bottom. She held the paint in one hand. She put her other hand on the tree trunk as she climbed up again.

I saw her start to slip. But I could not reach her fast enough. It was only a couple of feet down to the bottom. But she fell all the way.

60

"Ouch! Ouch!" she wailed.

Alicia sat on the ground, crying.

"Are you okay?" called Bobby, running down the steps.

We all hurried down to see if she was hurt. Luckily she had only skinned her hand and banged her knee.

Bobby and I led Alicia into the house. Mommy took care of her bruises. Then we went back outside.

"You see, little kids can get hurt around here," I said. "From now on there is a new rule. No kids under six can play in the treehouse."

"No fair!" said Willie.

"Double no fair!" said Andrew.

Andrew, Alicia, Meghan, and Willie did not like my rule one bit. (Alicia even started to cry again.)

"They are right. It is not fair," said Nancy.

"Any one of us could have slipped," said Kathryn.

"Even you," said Bobby.

"I do not care," I replied. "No kids under six. That is the rule."

"Who made you boss of the treehouse?" asked Alicia, sniffling.

I shrugged.

"I am seven," I replied.

Everyone glared at me. The Treehouse War was on.

13

Back Where We Started

On Saturday morning, Mommy drove Andrew and me downtown. We were going to buy new shoes to replace the ones Sadie ate.

We were halfway down the block when we saw Mark and Eric walking Sadie. Actually, she was walking *them*. That is because Sadie was pulling so hard.

"Hi, everyone!" I called out the window. "See you later."

When we got back from our shopping trip, Mommy dropped us off at the Bartons' house. All five kids were in the front yard playing with Sadie. Sadie was so happy to see Andrew and me, she almost knocked us over.

"Is everyone having a good time with Sadie?" I asked.

"We were having fun," said Eric. "But I thought you told us she was a little bit trained."

"She is," I replied. "She knows how to sit. And she knows to come if you call her."

"No, she does not," said Meghan. "We call her all the time. Watch."

The five Barton kids called Sadie at once. The problem was they were standing in different places. Sadie did not know where to go. She looked confused.

"Only one of you can call her at a time. You do it like this," I said. "Sadie, come!"

Sadie looked at me. Finally, she trotted to me.

"Let me try it," said Mark. "Sadie, come!"

Sadie looked in Mark's direction. Then

Meghan and Lynda started arguing about a toy. They were on the other side of the yard. Sadie looked their way. Eric and Jackie started giggling about something. They were standing in a different direction altogether. Sadie looked confused. Poor Sadie.

"Maybe you could skip training her now. You could just have fun with her," I said.

We tried playing a game of fetch. But the Barton kids kept throwing different toys to Sadie. So she just lay down and did not fetch any.

"Come on, Karen. We have to go," said Andrew.

It was time for lunch so Andrew and I headed home. While we were eating, the phone rang. Seth went to the den to answer it. He came back a few minutes later. He did not look too happy.

"That was Mr. Barton," said Seth. "He does not think Sadie is doing very well with so many kids around. She will not listen to anyone. And she just threw up her lunch."

"What do they want to do?" asked Mommy.

"They want to give her back to us," replied Seth. "The kids are coming over to work on the treehouse this afternoon. I told Mr. Barton to send Sadie over with them."

Oh, boy. We were back where we started. I jumped up from the table.

"Excuse me," I said.

"Karen, where are you going in such a hurry?" asked Mommy.

"I am going to hide my new shoes," I replied.

14

Bad to Worse

Sadie came galloping back into our yard. The first thing she did was make a puddle on our woodpile.

"No way!" I said. "We are having enough trouble building this treehouse without any help from you."

I led her inside and handed the leash to Seth.

Outside I found more trouble. This time it was the little kids. They had climbed up the trunk of the tree. They were painting pictures on the treehouse. Meanie-mo pic-

68

tures. One of them showed horns and claws — and pink glasses!

"Hey, what are you doing?" I asked.

"You told us we could not play *in* the treehouse. But you did not say we could not play outside it," said Willie.

"Then I am changing the rule. No kids under six *near* the treehouse," I replied.

The little kids started whispering to each other. Then they started giggling. But they climbed down from the tree.

I called a meeting for the rest of us.

"We need to watch the little kids. We have to make sure they follow the rule and do not get hurt," I said.

"It is your rule, Karen. It is not ours," said Nancy.

"We do not even like the rule," said Bobby.

"Why not? Alicia got hurt. Wouldn't you feel bad if another little kid got hurt?" I asked.

"Well, yes," replied Jackie. "Maybe Karen is right."

"No way. They could get hurt even if they are not playing at the treehouse. Any of us could," said Mark.

"You are just being bossy," said Lynda.

"I think Karen is trying to be nice," said Eric.

"Maybe. Maybe not," said Kathryn. "We should take a vote."

Goody. I love taking votes.

"All in favor of Karen's Rule, say aye. Aye!" I shouted.

But nobody else could decide.

"Aye, um, no wait. I take it back," said Eric.

"Aye . . . I'm not sure," said Nancy.

"Aye. No, not aye. Yes, aye. No, not aye. Oh, I do not know what to do," said Kathryn.

"We can keep the rule today since the little kids are gone anyway," I said. "We can take another vote tomorrow."

"That is the best idea," said Nancy. "We are wasting time arguing. We need to finish painting."

Everyone agreed to go back to work. We marched over to our paints.

"Where did the brushes go?" asked Bobby.

We heard giggling from behind some bushes. The little kids jumped out and called, "Finders keepers, losers weepers!"

I stomped over to the bushes. Now I was mad. Things were going from bad to worse.

"Where are those brushes, Andrew Brewer?" I said.

"I'm not telling," said Andrew with a big grin.

"Where are the brushes, Alicia?" asked Bobby.

"I am not telling, either."

"Willie, where are the brushes?" asked Kathryn.

Willie covered his mouth and did not answer.

"Meghan?" asked Lynda.

"If you want them, you have to find them."

That did it. The big kids started shouting.

The little kids shouted back. Then they started crying.

The next thing we knew Sadie was in the middle of everything. So was Seth.

"Quiet down, everyone," said Seth. "Someone please tell me what is going on."

An Important Phone Call

We all started talking at once. We told Seth about my rule. We told him what the little kids did to us. We told him about our vote.

"Whoa," said Seth. "I think I see the problem. I think the problem is me. I have been so busy with Sadie that I have not been helping enough with the treehouse."

"We are good at some things. But I guess we could use a little help with other things," I replied.

"I would like to see what you've done so

far," said Seth. "But first I would like to hear some apologies. There was a lot of yelling out here a few minutes ago."

"I am not sure I want to apologize," said Andrew.

"Me, neither," said Alicia.

"Then I do not want to apologize either," I said.

"About this rule, Karen," said Seth. "I plan to be around more. And we can fix up the treehouse to make it as safe as possible. So do you think we will need the rule?"

"I guess not," I replied.

"Good. Then we can start fresh. The best way to start fresh is with apologies. Whoever apologizes say aye," Seth said.

"Aye!" we all replied.

We led Seth to our treehouse. We showed him our railings and painted walls. (The little kids promised to paint over their meanie-mo pictures.)

"I think these railings are great. We can add a few planks of wood going across as a safety feature. That way no one can get stuck between the railings," said Seth. He looked my way and smiled.

We agreed to add ropes to our ladder so we'd have something to hang on to when we climbed up. (The big kids can climb up very well without ropes. But I knew ropes would be good for the little kids.)

"All we will have left is the roof. You kids have done a terrific job without me," said Seth.

"Seth, will you come here, please?" called Mommy. "We have an important phone call."

I wondered what it could be. I found out soon enough. Mommy and Seth were heading toward the car.

"Let's go, kids," said Seth. "A woman named Mrs. Gillen just phoned to say that she and her husband may have found Midgie."

Midgie! I could hardly believe my ears. None of the other people who thought they had Midgie really did. But maybe this time. Maybe these people really had found her!

"See you later," I said to my friends.

Andrew and I raced to the car.

"Please let it be Midgie. Please, please, please," I whispered to myself.

I closed my eyes and whispered the same thing over and over again.

"What are you saying?" asked Andrew.

I told him. We both started saying it out loud. Then Mommy and Seth joined in.

By the time we reached the couple's house, we were all chanting together. "Please let it be Midgie. Please, please, please!"

16

Midgie!

I was the first one out of the car. I raced to the door and rang the bell. I could hear barking inside. It sounded awfully familiar.

An elderly man opened the door. Guess who was standing beside him.

"Midgie!" I shouted.

I could tell she was happy to see me. She was not just wagging her tail. She was wagging her whole body.

I scooped her up in my arms and hugged her. My family raced to us.

"Thank you so much, Mr. Gillen," said

Seth. "I can see you have taken very good care of Midgie."

An elderly woman joined us.

"I am Mrs. Gillen," she said. "Please come in and sit down. I am sure you would like to hear how Midgie has been."

"Thank you," said Mommy. "We would love to."

We sat down in the Gillens' living room.

"Look at all these dog toys," I said. "Midgie, are you sure you want to come home with us?"

Mr. and Mrs. Gillen laughed.

"We have tried our best to make her happy," said Mr. Gillen. "We found her about two and a half weeks ago. Her collar and tags were missing. We thought she must be a stray and took her in."

"We kept our eyes open for signs in the neighborhood. But we don't go too far from home these days. So we did not see any," said Mrs. Gillen.

"This morning I had an appointment with my doctor," continued Mr. Gillen.

"That is when we saw your sign. It was posted on his street."

"Thank you for calling us as soon as you did," said Mommy.

"And thank you again for taking such good care of Midgie," said Seth.

"We were afraid something terrible had happened to her," I said.

Midgie was sitting between Andrew and me. We did not want to let her out of our sight.

"May I get you something to drink?" asked Mrs. Gillen.

"No, you have done enough already," said Seth. "You have also gone to some expense to take care of Midgie. May I pay you back for her food and toys?"

"Absolutely not," said Mr. Gillen. "It was a pleasure to have her with us. We are going to miss her."

"You can come visit her anytime," I said.

Mr. and Mrs. Gillen gave us the toys they had bought for Midgie. They each gave her a hug.

We piled into the car with Midgie and headed home.

"Now Midgie will get to meet Sadie!" said Andrew on the way.

"You are right," replied Seth. "I almost forgot Sadie was back with us."

"There is something else we cannot forget," I said. "Somehow Midgie escaped from our house. We have to find out how. Otherwise, she might do it again."

17

Case Closed

The little house had turned into a little zoo. We had Midgie, Sadie, Rocky, Emily Junior, and Bob.

The good news was that Midgie and Sadie got along fine. The bad news was that Sadie and Rocky still had to be kept apart. And Sadie was still a lot of work.

"Uh-oh. Somebody better come outside!" called Andrew from the yard.

Mommy and Seth had let Andrew take Sadie in the backyard for a minute. We hurried to see what had happened.

"The leash slipped out of my hand and she knocked over the can of paint," said Andrew. "Then she slipped in it."

Sadie was covered with green paint. Andrew had paint all over his hands and pants and shoes.

"I will clean up Sadie," said Seth.

"I will help Andrew," said Mommy. "We have got to find a new home for Sadie. She is too much work when we already have so many pets."

While everyone was busy cleaning up, I did another important job.

"Midgie, your disappearing days are over," I said. "I am going to find out how you have been escaping."

I decided to search our house from the top all the way down. The attic door was locked. So Midgie was not getting out that way.

I checked each of the bedrooms and the bathroom to make sure no windows were open. She could have climbed out an open window and then gone down a tree. Maybe.

But the windows were closed or open just a crack. Midgie could not have been getting out that way either.

I checked the first floor. Midgie was standing outside the basement door yapping to get downstairs.

Hmm. I rememberd that she had been doing that a lot before she ran away.

"Stay here, Midgie," I said. "I am going down to the basement to investigate."

I opened the basement door and closed it quickly so Midgie could not follow me. I checked each of the two big windows. They were shut tight. I checked the floorboards to make sure that none were loose. Then I checked the small window over the refrigerator. The latch was broken. I gently pushed the window frame. The window opened. It was just big enough for Midgie to fit through. But it was awfully high.

I stood back and sized up the situation. If Midgie were to jump onto the chair, then onto the washing machine, then onto the top of the refrigerator . . .

"Aha! Midgie would be free," I said.

The case of the disappearing dog was closed. I ran upstairs to tell everyone the news. (I made sure to shut the basement door behind me.)

"You are an amazing detective!" said Seth. "I am going to fix the window lock right this minute."

"I will help you," I said. "We do not want Midgie to run away ever again."

18

Special Delivery

Me-ow! Me-ow! Woof! Woof! Woof! Me-ow!
It was Sunday. We were trying to eat a peaceful family lunch. Mommy jumped up from her chair and headed for the living room.

"I thought Sadie was under your chair, Seth," she said.

"So did I," replied Seth, jumping up after Mommy.

When they came back, they were carrying Sadie. They closed the door so Rocky could not get in.

"We have to be more careful about keeping them apart," said Mommy. "And we have to do something about finding Sadie a new home."

"We will put up signs and place an ad in the paper," replied Seth.

"No, wait! I have a better idea," I said. "The Gillens were very good pet owners. Maybe they would like to take Sadie."

"Oh, no. They are too old for Sadie. She is way too much work," Mommy replied.

"But the Gillens do not have any other pets," I said. "Or kids. Their yard is fenced in. And they *loved* having Midgie."

"It is certainly worth a phone call," said Seth.

"All right," agreed Mommy. "Let's give it a try."

Seth called Mr. and Mrs. Gillen. He told them about Sadie. But the Gillens did not want to take her. They said Midgie was one thing. A puppy was another.

Boo and bullfrogs.

"I think it is time to make our signs,"

said Mommy. "I am sure someone in the neighborhood would love a puppy like Sadie. She is a lot of trouble now, but she will grow up to be a wonderful dog."

I helped clear the table. Then we made our sign. It said:

BEAUTIFUL GOLDEN RETRIEVER PUPPY NEEDS LOVING HOME

We put a picture of Sadie in the middle and our phone number at the bottom.

Just as we finished making the sign, the phone rang. Seth answered it and came back with a big smile on his face.

"We are not going to need that sign after all," he said. "That was the Gillens. They have changed their minds. They would like to take Sadie. They remembered how sweet Midgie is. And how much she made them laugh. And how many new friends they made when they walked her. They really want to have a dog around. In fact, they said they wanted Sadie more than anything in the world."

"That is terrific news!" said Mommy.

"Hooray!" I said.

I looked at our beautiful sign. It was too bad no one would see it. But I was happy the Gillens were going to take Sadie.

"I offered to drive Sadie over to their house," said Seth. "We can all ride there together."

I packed up the toys Mr. and Mrs. Gillen had bought for Midgie. Now they would be Sadie's toys. Then we piled into our car. Andrew and I hugged Sadie.

"You will be happy with the Gillens," I told her. "They have a fenced-in yard. And you will be their only pet."

When we arrived at the Gillens' house, I held Sadie's leash and Andrew rang the bell.

"Special delivery!" I called.

"She looks so sweet!" said Mrs. Gillen when she opened the door and saw Sadie.

She reached out to pet her. Sadie was so

excited she made a puddle. I was glad we were still outside.

"This puppy will keep us young," said Mr. Gillen.

I handed him the leash and the bag of toys. I felt sad. But I felt relieved, too.

"Be good, Sadie," said Andrew.

"Be happy, Sadie," I said.

We took turns hugging Sadie good-bye. Then we headed home.

19

No Grown-ups Allowed

Andrew and I gathered everyone together to work on the treehouse.

"Let's get this building crew working!"
said Seth.

He was in a very good mood. That is
because Midgie was home and Sadie had a
brand-new family.

The first thing we did was put the roof
on our treehouse. That way it would be
cozy even in the rain. We made an assembly line. Seth called out what he needed.
We passed it to him.

"Board!" called Seth.

"Board!" we all answered.

The board went from hand to hand. (When the boards were big, two little kids had to hold them at once. I worried they might drop one on their toes and get hurt. But I was very good. I did not say one word.)

It took awhile. But finally the roof was finished. Seth said he would paint the outside for us. We took a vote and decided on blue. It was our job to paint the inside.

"Let's make it look like the sky," I said. "That would be pretty."

"We could paint the moon and the stars," said Kathryn.

"I want to paint a sun," said Willie.

"Let's paint everything!" I said.

That is what we did. We painted stars, clouds, birds, the moon, the sun, an airplane, a rocket ship, a kite, and a lost balloon. It was a very busy sky.

By the time we finished, my hair was

about six different colors. That is because I put too much paint on my brush and it dripped down on my head.

"That ceiling looks fantastic, kids," said Seth. "We can leave it to dry overnight and finish up tomorrow."

My friends and I got together again after school on Monday. Our house looked gigundoly beautiful. But it was gigundoly empty, too.

"We need to decorate," I said. "Who has furniture?"

"We have a table and a few chairs in our attic," said Jackie. "We never use them anymore."

"My parents just put an old trunk down in the basement," said Nancy. "I bet we could have that."

There was something in our basement I wanted, too. I would have to ask Mommy if I could have it.

We went to our houses and came back with whatever we were allowed to have.

Mommy let me have the thing I wanted most. It was a big straw basket we used to use for laundry.

"We can hang this from the treehouse with ropes," I told my friends. "Then we can send things up and down."

We had the basket. We had the Bartons' table and chairs. (They were light so it was easy to haul them up to the treehouse.) Nancy's trunk made a great treasure chest. We had a mirror. A rug. Two old telephones. A painting of a clown and one of a cat.

It took a long time to attach the basket so it went up and down without getting stuck. But we did it. By the time we were finished, we had a real and true treehouse.

We ran to get our parents so they could see it. They took turns climbing up the steps.

"It is beautiful!" said Mommy.

"And so cozy," said Kathryn's mother.

"May I hide out here sometimes?" asked Bobby's father.

"No!" we all replied.

"We are sorry, Mr. Gianelli. No grown-ups allowed," I said.

I knew I was making up another rule without asking. But I do not think anyone minded. Except the grown-ups. They looked disappointed. My friends and I would have to put up a sign that said *No Grown-ups Allowed*. Otherwise one of the grown-ups might forget.

Our treehouse was a special place. We had built it ourselves. Okay, Seth helped a little. But it was ours. And it was for kids only.

20

Welcome Back, Midgie

When I got home from school on Tuesday, Mommy said the Gillens had called. For a moment I felt worried. But everything was fine. The Gillens just wanted to let us know how much they were enjoying Sadie.

Woof, woof! Meow! Woof, woof! Meow!

Midgie was chasing Rocky around the house. But with the window fixed, we knew she could not escape again. It was time for a celebration.

Andrew and I ate our after school snack, then went outside. Our friends were arriving at the treehouse one by one.

"Listen up, everyone. I have an idea," I said when they had all arrived. "I think we should have a party in our new treehouse. It could be a 'Welcome Back, Midgie' party."

I did not even have to take a vote. Everyone liked my idea.

My friends and I are very good at throwing parties. It did not take long for us to get ready. We each went home and returned with bags filled with things for the party. We had plenty of food: apples, raisins, potato chips, pretzels, juice, and soda for us, and dog biscuits for Midgie. We had party hats and noisemakers. (Midgie did not know how to blow on a noisemaker. But there was a hat for her to wear.) We decorated our treehouse with balloons and streamers. And we had a welcome home gift for Midgie. It was an excellent stick for playing fetch.

"Will Midgie be able to walk up our ladder?" asked Nancy.

"She will not have to," I replied. "She is small enough to fit in the basket. We can pull her up to the party!"

Everything was ready. The only thing left to do was bring out the guest of honor.

I went inside and put Midgie on her leash. I put a party hat on her head. Then I led her outside.

Everyone clapped and cheered for Midgie.

"Welcome back, Midgie," said Andrew. "You will not run away again, will you?"

Woof! replied Midgie.

We put the basket on the ground and helped Midgie into it. The basket was just Midgie's size. Midgie sat down inside.

The three biggest kids in our group are Eric, Mark, and Jackie. They climbed into the treehouse and grabbed the rope.

I followed them with Nancy and Bobby to help Midgie out when the basket came up.

The rest of the kids stayed on the ground cheering Midgie on.

"One, two, three, pull!" called Mark.

The basket rose a little higher with each pull. The treehouse is not very far off the ground, so Midgie would not get hurt if she jumped out. But she liked the basket. She sat inside and enjoyed the ride.

"One, two, three, pull!" called Mark for the last time.

I reached in and lifted Midgie out of the basket. Nancy and Bobby helped.

"Our guest of honor has arrived!" I announced.

The rest of the kids climbed up, too. We presented Midgie with her stick. (I had tied a red bow on it.) Then we sang a welcome back cheer.

"Two, four, six, eight, who do we appreciate? Midgie! Midgie! Hooray!"

Woof! Woof! barked Midgie.

I gave her a dog biscuit and a hug.

"Welcome back, Midgie," I said. "I am glad you are home."

About the Author

ANN M. MARTIN lives in New York City and loves animals, especially cats. She has two cats of her own, Gussie and Woody.

Other books by Ann M. Martin that you might enjoy are *Stage Fright*; *Me and Katie (the Pest)*; and the books in *The Baby-sitters Club* series.

Ann likes ice cream and *I Love Lucy*. And she has her own little sister, whose name is Jane.

Little Sister

Don't miss #73

KAREN'S DINOSAUR

I could not believe my eyes. I decided the museum was one of the best places I had ever visited. I thought about David Michael. I knew he would think it was one of the best places *he* had ever visited, too. (I felt a little bad about that.)

"Time to begin your projects now," said Mrs. Hoffman.

Maxie and I went with Mrs. Hoffman to the other hall.

"I hope ornitholestes is here," I said to Maxie.

"Me, too," she agreed.

We began to look.

We checked every single display. And soon we found it.

"Look!" exclaimed Maxie. "A skeleton, a whole skeleton."

LITTLE 🍎 APPLE®

BABY SITTERS
Little Sister™

by Ann M. Martin,
author of The Baby-sitters Club ®

☐	MQ44300-3	#1	Karen's Witch	$2.95
☐	MQ44259-7	#2	Karen's Roller Skates	$2.95
☐	MQ44299-7	#3	Karen's Worst Day	$2.95
☐	MQ44264-3	#4	Karen's Kittycat Club	$2.95
☐	MQ44258-9	#5	Karen's School Picture	$2.95
☐	MQ44298-8	#6	Karen's Little Sister	$2.95
☐	MQ44257-0	#7	Karen's Birthday	$2.95
☐	MQ42670-2	#8	Karen's Haircut	$2.95
☐	MQ43652-X	#9	Karen's Sleepover	$2.95
☐	MQ43651-1	#10	Karen's Grandmothers	$2.95
☐	MQ43650-3	#11	Karen's Prize	$2.95
☐	MQ43649-X	#12	Karen's Ghost	$2.95
☐	MQ43648-1	#13	Karen's Surprise	$2.95
☐	MQ43646-5	#14	Karen's New Year	$2.95
☐	MQ43645-7	#15	Karen's in Love	$2.95
☐	MQ43644-9	#16	Karen's Goldfish	$2.95
☐	MQ43643-0	#17	Karen's Brothers	$2.95
☐	MQ43642-2	#18	Karen's Home-Run	$2.75
☐	MQ43641-4	#19	Karen's Good-Bye	$2.95
☐	MQ44823-4	#20	Karen's Carnival	$2.95
☐	MQ44824-2	#21	Karen's New Teacher	$2.95
☐	MQ44833-1	#22	Karen's Little Witch	$2.95
☐	MQ44832-3	#23	Karen's Doll	$2.95
☐	MQ44859-5	#24	Karen's School Trip	$2.95
☐	MQ44831-5	#25	Karen's Pen Pal	$2.95
☐	MQ44830-7	#26	Karen's Ducklings	$2.95
☐	MQ44829-3	#27	Karen's Big Joke	$2.95
☐	MQ44828-5	#28	Karen's Tea Party	$2.95
☐	MQ44825-0	#29	Karen's Cartwheel	$2.75
☐	MQ45645-8	#30	Karen's Kittens	$2.95
☐	MQ45646-6	#31	Karen's Bully	$2.95
☐	MQ45647-4	#32	Karen's Pumpkin Patch	$2.95
☐	MQ45648-2	#33	Karen's Secret	$2.95
☐	MQ45650-4	#34	Karen's Snow Day	$2.95
☐	MQ45652-0	#35	Karen's Doll Hospital	$2.95
☐	MQ45651-2	#36	Karen's New Friend	$2.95
☐	MQ45653-9	#37	Karen's Tuba	$2.95
☐	MQ45655-5	#38	Karen's Big Lie	$2.95
☐	MQ45654-7	#39	Karen's Wedding	$2.95
☐	MQ47040-X	#40	Karen's Newspaper	$2.95
☐	MQ47041-8	#41	Karen's School	$2.95
☐	MQ47042-6	#42	Karen's Pizza Party	$2.95
☐	MQ46912-6	#43	Karen's Toothache	$2.95

More Titles... ➡